Aloha!
Betty Daniel

With my best regards!
Bernard Atkins

To Holly
With love
Grandpa & Grandma
1997

PRINCE POLOKA
OF ULI LOKO

story by **Becky Daniel**
pictures by **Bernard Atkins**

Dedication

To those courageous enough
to begin the journey--especially
the lucky few who return home again.

Hawaiian-English

aloha	ah **lo** hah	hello
Hu 'a Loko	**hoo** ah **low** ko	Scum Pond
(King) Pupuka	poo **poo** kah	ugly
ku'oko'a	koo **oh** ko **ah**	freedom
makamakas.	**mah** kah **mah** kahs	friends
(Queen) Lani	**lah** nee	sky
'Ohana	oh **hah** nah	family
(Prince) Poloka	poh **low** kah	frog
(Princess) Pua	**poo** ah	flower
Uli Loko	**oo** lee **low** ko	Blue Lake

© 1994 Becky Daniel & Bernard Atkins
Published by Great Creations

Aloha. I am Prince Poloka. This is my Hawaiian home, Uli Loko (Blue Lake). I have a story to share with you. Like many stories with happy endings, mine had a sad beginning.

Once upon a time I shared Uli Loko with my ʻohana
(family). Then the frog catchers came and caught them all--
my father the king, my mother, and my brothers and
sisters. I was the only one who escaped the great net. For
days I hopped from lily pad to lily pad in search of another
survivor. Weeks passed, then months. I was too sad to swim,
too unhappy to eat.

Finally I decided that I had to leave Uli Loko. I thought to myself, "I'll go in search of some great treasures and seek my fortune in a happier place. Then perhaps I can fill the emptiness in my heart."

The next morning I feasted on fat flies.

I put on my most princely clothes and hopped into the lush tropical forest.

But after hopping most of the day, I began to worry.
What if I can't find food? What if my skin dries out and there
is no water? What if I die! I was too tired to go on.

Then suddenly the sun disappeared behind a dark cloud. Big drops of rain splashed down and cooled my hot skin and brought squirmy worms and fat slugs from their hiding places. Dinner!

With my little green body and my great big hopes both renewed, I hopped on down the path until the sunset turned the sky pink and scarlet.

When the moon rose high over the islands and cast its pearly light upon the ferns and flowers of the forest, I was fast asleep.

The next day I hadn't traveled far before I heard a familiar sound, "Rib-bit. Rib-bit." That was the sound I make.

Looking through a curtain of green leaves, I saw lots of frogs!
Too many to count! Frogs, frogs, and more frogs jammed into
a tiny, murky pond. Others waited their turn on the narrow
bank. One look at the skinny frogs and I knew there weren't
enough flies to go around. It was plain to see that there were
no treasures to be found here.

I saw a dozen frogs in uniforms marching around the pond. One of them saw me and demanded, "Halt! Who goes there?"

"I am Prince Poloka of Uli Loko," I answered. "I'm on my way to find great treasures."

Suddenly two marchers grabbed me from behind and dragged me off to their leader.

They shoved me in front of a big, fat frog. "King Pupuka, we found this stranger by the pond. He wants to steal our treasures," said one marcher.

The king's long, sticky tongue snapped out and caught a buzzing fly. He chomped several times and smacked his lips.

Croaking with glee, the marchers closed in and poked their sticks at me. All at once I realized that I was in danger.

King Pupuka glared at me. "Who are you?" he demanded.

"I am Prince Poloka of Uli Loko," I said.

"A prince? You call yourself a prince? You are not my son; therefore, you are not a prince."

How could I show these frogs that I truly was a prince and not a thief? "I am prince of another place," I answered softly.

"What! Another place? There is no other place! This is Hu'a Loko (Scum Pond), the only place!" bellowed the king.
"You are right, King Pupuka, I'm not your son," I said.

The king rocked back on his stone throne as green heads bobbed approval.

"But I am here. Therefore, I must have come from another place," I told him.

"Indeed. Another place," said King Pupuka. His slimy eyelids closed over his bulging eyes. "Indeed!"

He paused a moment. His eyes flew open, "If you come from another place, give me proof!" Once more green heads bobbed.

King parted the circle of frogs, hopped a distance of three feet, faced me and demanded, "Tell me, is your home this big?"

When I turned in King's direction I saw a beautiful princess standing next to the queen.

"Answer me! Is your home this big?" King Pupuka demanded once again.

"Bigger." I couldn't stop staring at that green goddess. Who was she? For a moment I forgot all of my fears.

King hopped another three feet and shouted, "Is your home this big?"

"Far bigger than that," I said, staring into the most beautiful bulging eyes I had ever seen.

Furious and out of breath, he hopped back in front of me. "Do you dare suggest before the King of Hu'a Loko, Queen Lani, the fair Princess Pua, and all of my subjects here that your home is as big as Hu'a Loko?"

Then Princess Pua smiled at me. She was gorgeous! My courage grew, and I said, "Uli Loko is a huge, beautiful crystal-clear lake with swarms of fat, buzzing flies everywhere."

"And the beautiful paradise where I come from does not have one greedy, gobbling frog that eats most of the food while others are starving."

Looking at Princess Pua I added, "You are all welcome to come
back to Uli Loko with me."

"Liar! How dare you say that you come from a place bigger than Huʻa Loko. How dare you insult me and my vast kingdom! I am King Pupuka of Huʻa Loko, the only place. I banish you to Stench Bog!"

"Oh, no! Not Stench Bog," gasped the frog mob.

"Anything but the Bog," whispered Queen Lani, as she looked toward the darkest corner of Huʻa Loko.

"Guards, take him away," ordered the king.

The king's guards leaped forward to arrest me, but some of the other frogs bravely hopped between the guards and me.

"Let him prove his innocence by showing us this frog paradise," Princess Pua begged her father.

"Free him! Free him!" croaked a few brave frogs.

"Guards! Take him away!" ordered the king again.

"Guilty!" croaked King Pupuka's faithful guards.
"Guilty!" Then one of the guards poked me with his stick,
while another grabbed me and started pulling me away. Just
then one brave frog began to shout, "Kuʻokoʻa (Freedom)!"

Soon there was a croaking choir. "Kuʻokoʻa! Kuʻokoʻa!"

It was then that the great frog battle of Huʻa Loko broke out. I gathered Princess Pua in my arms and carried her safely outside the mob of fighting frogs.

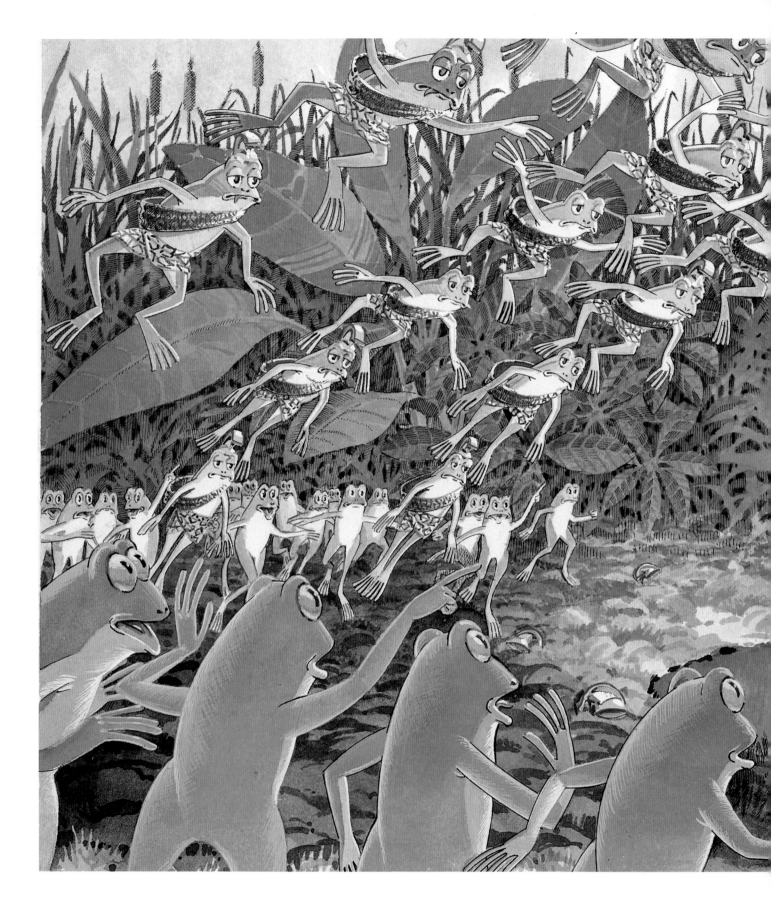

Soon the guards were being overpowered by the rest of the frogs. Fearing for his life, King Pupuka sprang high into the air and dove into Huʻa Loko.

One by one, as if attached to the king by invisible strings, each of his guards sprang high into the air and landed in the pond, too.

Kerplop! Kerplop! All landed right on top of King Pupuka. "Long live the king," gurgled from the pond.

Picking up sticks and stones, my followers surrounded the pile of dazed frogs. They began to close in. "Ku'oko'a, ku'oko'a!"

With Princess Pua by my side, I hopped up and stood on the king's stone throne. I raised one hand to silence the mob. "Stop! Good frogs," I begged. "Forgive your brothers. They do not dare to dream of a better place. Please stop."

As I spoke, I heard the princess sigh.

"You are the brave ones who have chosen a different place. Please don't begin your new life by taking the life of another." Looking into Princess Pua's eyes I continued, "Come away with me to Uli Loko. I offer you all a frog's paradise. Follow me."

Then I took Princess Pua's dainty, green hand, and together we hopped toward Uli Loko.

Believing that I was truly a prince from another place, and without a backward glance, the frogs followed us into the forest.

We journeyed in the moonlight. We did a dance of celebration and croaked a song of joy as we hopped through the early morning hours beneath twinkling stars.

At sunrise we reached the water's edge.

The frogs were overjoyed that they had found the courage to leave Huʻa Loko. Princess Pua was especially happy.

I was glad to be home in my beautiful Uli Loko, and I had brought back the best treasures of all--makamakas (friends)!